TURN RIGHT

AT

TOOLIGIE

DENNIS LIGHTFOOT

Cover photograph by author, 2025.
Expanded with Adobe Photoshop AI.
Esky image courtesy of Pixabay.

ISBN: 978-0-6455080-6-2

With thanks to…

Mary G for publishing assistance.

Phillip Jackson had always dreamed of breaking the poverty cycle that he was born into. His father was plagued by chronic health issues and unable to work due to this. Having to care for him, his mother was only able to work part-time at a local supermarket.

A week after his fifteenth birthday, his parents strongly suggested that he quit school and find some paid employment. This suited Phil perfectly as his attention span in the classroom was minimal. His mind was fixated on adventuring along beaches and roaming through the hills – being out in the freedom of nature.

Phil found employment in the spare parts department of a local car dealership. His job was to identify the part numbers of replacement items for the many makes and models of cars the dealership was selling. However, after six years of the unceasing stress of his job, and saving as much of his wages as he could, he realised that his modest weekly income would never make him a rich man. Inflation, rising costs, stagnant wages were constantly eroding his endeavour to save. By carefully managing what money he received, he was able to put down a deposit on a modest house in the town.

Phil had always hoped that good fortune would come his way. Occasionally he purchased an item at a jumble sale that was of value, then sold it for a profit. But that was a slow way to get rich. The possibility of winning a lottery or discovering a hidden treasure was always in the back of his mind. So, when he discovered an old Minelab 15000 metal detector at a deceased estate sale with a price he could afford, he seized the opportunity and bought it. Little did he know that buying this in-ground metal seeking device would change his life.

His dream of wealth was now one step closer. From that day on, many weekends were spent waving his new electronic gadget, back and forth across the soft sand of the local beaches in search of anything of value. Armed with a non-metallic spade and a plastic sieve, his first priority was to comb every square metre of the local shorelines. Four weekends of metal detecting resulted him uncovering from beneath the sandy surface, a few coins, a piece of cheap jewellery and an assortment of other items of little value. Most of the items he found However, were trash. Hair clasps, and a substantial amount of rusty metal bottle caps, and ring-pulls from aluminium drink cans.

However, on one occasion his detector did locate something very worth money. That particular item was a famous brand expensive gold watch. Unfortunately for Phil, the watch owner was still looking for his time piece and had spotted him detecting close to the area where he had lost it. As Phil moved in a grid pattern up and down the area, ears alert for that electronic signal of something buried in the sand. The man hovered over his every action like a shadow. When the detector suddenly went beep, beep, beep, the 'lossee' immediately rushed over and stood uncomfortably close to Phil's side, eager to see what had been identified by the machine. Running the sand through the sieve, Phil revealed the item creating the noisy electronic response.

In the bottom of the strainer was something gold and shiny. 'It's my watch! That's it, that's mine, that's it,' the bloke shouted with delight and before Phil could do anything he grabbed it from the sieve. 'Thanks mate,' the man said as he shook off the remaining sand. With a quick glance to check if the seconds hand was still rotating, he then slid 'his' watch back on his wrist. 'It is still working – here's something for your troubles,' he exclaimed as he pulled out his wallet and handed Phil a ten dollar note. Before Phil could say or do anything, he hightailed off the beach.

Phillip had often seen similar watches in jewellers' catalogues, advertised in the fifteen-hundred-dollar price bracket. 'Cheapskate prick! – Ten miserly dollars!' Phil bemoaned as he pocketed the note, then resumed waving his magic stick back and forth. Feeling slightly dejected, he wished that the watch owner was not present at the time, and he could have kept his find.

Apart from a few more trinkets, the ever-present bottle caps and a two-dollar coin, the watch was the only exciting find that was worth any real money that day. Finding such a valuable item, stimulated his imagination. The time had come for him to check the other beaches in other coastal towns in order to perhaps find that elusive treasure in the sand, waiting to be discovered. However, being able to many times retell the story of the watch and its miserly owner to the inquisitive people who often approached him while on the beach asking if he 'had found anything?' and his friends gave him greater satisfaction than the reward he was given by the tightwad watch owner.

More weekends passed. Many more beaches were searched without another 'high value' item being found. He realised that the chance of ever finding another expensive watch or something of similar value was low on the discovery percentage chart, of beach detecting. A dejected (but one that would never surrender) Phil conferred with his girlfriend Barbara. Barbara and Phil had fallen in love in high school. They had dated for almost four years after leaving school before she moved in to live with him.

'I've done over all of the nearby beaches without success. All I have to show for my effort is that small jar of coins and a handful of fishing sinkers. Perhaps my next step should be to try and find some gold!' he lamented to Barbara.

The heat of an Eyre Peninsula summer was in full swing. Keeping cool was a priority. For the following three weekends, he enjoyed the air-conditioned comfort of the local library. His aim was to read all the books he could, to find out where gold could possibly be found on Eyre Peninsula. Phil began searching for books with old maps that showed the locations where the early settlers had registered and dug mines. By gaining this new knowledge he had greater insight as to where he might start looking for those elusive nuggets. 'Three weekends well spent,' he mused as he replaced the batteries in his detector, making it ready for finding gold.

With the days of excessive heat now having passed, loaded with backpack, water bottle, broad brimmed hat and some sweets to nibble, and with Barbara's blessing, he was off to find his fortune.

A forty-five-minute drive from Port Lincoln to the Tumby Bay foothills, and armed with a good dose of naïve enthusiasm and his lower end of the market detector, young Phil traipsed through the scrub to locate the first and closest mine on his list. It had been shown on a map as being a historic mine, dug in the late 1800s. What he found at the location was nothing more than a three-metre-deep hole in the ground. Seems the 'miners' had found some surface quartz. Hoping it was gold-bearing, they kept digging until all the quartz seam had been removed. There was nothing to indicate that any gold had ever been found. Not to be discouraged he clambered down into the hole and waved his detector back and forth over the walls and floor of that shallow mine. Not even a single blip came from his 'Gold Seeker magic stick'.

'Might as well do the outer area over while I'm here,' he muttered to himself as he climbed out of the 'mine'. Back and forth he eagerly swept his detector over the ground surrounding what had proven to be, just a pit. Several pieces of rusty wire and a few old, rusted cans were the only items he unearthed. 'One mine down, six more to go,' he said to himself as he was about to give up and head homeward. With the detector still switched on and lowered to the ground, he began walking back to his vehicle. Beep, beep, beep, screamed from his machine.

The sudden thrill of hearing such a strong signal stirred him into action. An invigorated urgency had him scraping away the soil, dumping each spade full in small separate piles alongside the hole he was digging. He continued waving his detector to and fro over the hole. Beep, beep, each time. More soil scraping until finally the beeps ceased from inside the hole. Now, the item would be on the surface in one of the little piles of dug out soil. A quick wave across each heap soon revealed the one containing his 'prize'. The sieve was now brought into action.

'Well look at that,' he said proudly as he lifted out an old copper coin. After a bit of spittle and a quick rub on his shirt, the date of it could be identified. 1897. It was an old English penny, probably not worth much. Nevertheless, Phil was delighted with his find.

The penny had boosted his enthusiasm to search further afield. The burning sting of the summer sun, gradually became a gentle autumn glow. Cooler days allowed him many more hours on weekends, to drive to remote locations, checking out other listed mine sites. From time to time, he would also see an area that possibly may contain the precious golden metal. Quartz reefs were known to often contain gold. They were of special interest and would be eagerly explored with the detector. However, nothing sent his detector into a 'Eureka' mode.

Phil continued to be employed by the local auto-parts dealer and spent many hours each day inside the warehouse, checking item numbers on a computer screen, packing parts into shelves and cartons, living his life under fluorescent lights. All spare parts departments are also known as being a stressful workplace, where everything was wanted, yesterday.

Even though Phil liked living with his girlfriend, he also enjoyed being on his own. Barbara worked at a local supermarket and was often called in on weekends. Before he purchased the detector, his weekends were sometimes spent without her. Barbara was in love with 'her man' and was happy to see him doing what he liked best – treasure hunting. She gave him full approval for his adventuring.

Being alone, out in the sunshine and the Aussie bush re-energized Phil's spirit and greatly reduced his workplace-induced stress levels. Surrounded by clean fresh air with little more than the chirp of the local birdlife and occasionally sighting of a lizard scurry back under a rock gave him immense satisfaction and made his boring working-life worth doing. However, there was a cost burden in the need to travel. Paying for fuel was always the downside the adventurous young fellow had to contend with. Rising fuel prices forced Phil to rethink his 'gold search' strategy and find ways to reduce his expenditure or do less travelling.

His astute eye had notice that everywhere he ventured the occasional old bottle or glass jar were there for the taking. Plus, there were returnable deposit-unit bottles and cans that had been discarded. These were now litter, left behind in the scrub by those who were too slack to take them back home for proper disposal. Collecting and returning the bottles and cans for recycle, he realised could be an added cash bonus to offset part of his fuel expenses.

Several weekends of detecting went by without finding one speck of the precious yellow metal. Phil had to now accept that the lower Eyre Peninsula was devoid of any gold, and the old mines marked on maps had never become anything more than holes in the ground. He was doubtful that any of the listed mines produced any golden metal worth the effort of digging.

The time had come for Phil's outdoor adventures to change. It had become boring to be waving the Minelab detector across acres of on unyielding dirt, only finding only pieces of wire and other rusty worthless metal objects.

After a few weeks of staying home, his yearning to be out in the bush made him restless. He suggested to Barbara they go camping together. 'And who is going to wash our clothes and do the house-cleaning if we do?' she replied and laughed. 'I am happy for you to go scrub bashing. Why don't you now go out and collect the discarded the bottles and cans strewn about in the scrub you told me about. You never know, you might find some old ones that collectors are seeking.'

What started out as beach detecting, then searching for elusive gold, gradually morphed into a serious obsession of bottle collecting. His approach to treasure searching now had a different objective – old glassware. It wasn't long before he had accumulated many vintage bottles and jars of all shapes, colours and sizes, that he had found in the same areas he previously searched, but this time with his eyes concentrating on a new target. Apart from the many 'return for deposit' units, occasionally he would unearth an old bottle of some value, eagerly sought by collectors. One particular find was of much interest. It was an early 1920s light green, rare, Port Augusta cool drink bottle, with an elaborate embossed logo. Using his computer he tracked down one of the same make and vintage. Eighty five dollars was the listed price.

'Wow! Who would have thought that just one old bottle would be worth that much,' he told his computer screen.

Now the metal detector only went along for the ride, staying in the vehicle, during his scrub walking adventures. Plastic shopping bags were carried in his backpack instead of the plastic sieve and spare batteries for the detector. A new era of enthusiasm had arrived.

The many National Parks on Eyre Peninsula's occupied huge

expanses of scrubland. Each Park was worthy of seeking out where the old timers had once passed, droving cattle, herding their sheep, and where government surveyors, rabbit trappers and 'roo shooters eked out a living. Amidst the scrub, they would also make camp. Sometimes just an over-nighter but often a more permanent camp where they would stay for week or more.

Phil was a born bushman and had no fear of being alone miles away from the nearest town. One rule he had, was to park his faithful old four door Rodeo ute, discretely tucked safely out of sight, in order not to advertise his presence in the area, whilst he hunted for those campsites and search for the elusive piece of antique glassware.

Phil soon realised that rusty cans and campfire ashes were the obvious sign of an old campsite. Around such places, he would walk a circular grid search pattern. Often finding bottles or other item that had been discarded by the campers.

On one occasion whilst he was doing a grid search, he heard a car approaching. As the sound of the vehicle came closer he discretely watched between the trees, catching a glimpse of a green ute, with only the driver inside, pass nearby. Being in the Hinks Conservation Reserve at least three kilometres from the Tod Highway and down a remote sandy track, it puzzled him as to where the vehicle was headed. Phil sensed that due to the driver's haste, he may have been in the area before and knew exactly where he was going.

A bird watcher perhaps – but who would be in this particular area that had very little interesting birdlife, apart from the rare Mallee Fowl? His ears continued to follow the sound of its motor. It wasn't long before it stopped somewhere in the scrub. From the close proximity of the last sound, it would have only been a few hundred metres away from where Phil was standing. His curiosity got the better of him. Finding the car would be simple. All he had to do was to walk back out onto the track and follow the vehicles tyre marks left in the dry sand.

It was not long before he found where the car had turned off from the open track and onto a side trail. Even though the soft sandy soil muffled the sound of his footsteps he walked stealthily, following the cars wheel marks. About 100 metres along the trail he spotted the car cleverly concealed among a thicket of Mallee trees. Whoever was driving that vehicle was also trying to hide their whereabouts. Phil could now identify the car as a current model green Toyota Hilux dual cab Ute. One that he had not seen in the area ever before. 'Why would someone do that'? He thought. Then chuckled to himself, 'I always hide my car, suppose they can do the same.'

Staying close to the bushes Phil crept closer. When he was about twenty metres from the Hilux he could see the driver was not in the vehicle, nor anywhere nearby. Fearing he would be seen he moved away to a dense clump of Mallee, then crouched down behind the leafiest section and waited. His ears strained, listening for the sound of someone moving about.

Almost ten minutes had passed before he heard a person walking through the bushes and advancing in the direction of the Ute. A rather sweaty, thickset, bearded man of Middle Eastern appearance carrying a shovel appeared. As he neared the car he looked cautiously around as though he was ensuring that no one had seen him. He clicked his remote locking device, opened the rear passenger door placed the spade in behind the driver's seat.

Then opened the front driver's side door, climbed in. For a while he sat peering down at what Phil assumed was a mobile phone. After a few minutes he started the engine then reversed the vehicle out of its concealed location, did a three-point turn and drove back down the track.

'What in the hell was he up to?' Phil muttered to himself as he emerged from his hidey-spot. Where had he been? What was he doing out in this remote place?

'This needs further investigation,' he said to himself. He advanced to where the Hilux Ute had been parked and decided to retrace the foot tracks made by the man.

Following shoe tracks should have been just as easy as following tyre tracks, However, the footprints he followed further into the scrub disappeared when they turned into a rocky outcrop section.

'Clever bastard,' Phil cursed. Despite searching the area for another thirty minutes nothing could be found to indicate what the chap was doing. 'Perhaps he just went for a crap,' Phil silently laughed to himself. He remained perplexed as to why would somebody come so far off the highway, and hide their car, if they were simply going to the toilet.

Phil pondered several scenarios. Maybe he had buried a dog or a cat, or maybe set some traps for rabbits, or set a camera to record wildlife. Over the years he had seen pet lovers do strange things when their beloved companions died. Back yard burials with little wooden crosses were most common, but other odd interments were often the case. Owners would bury their deceased pets near favourite walking spots or under a certain tree. Perhaps another search on another day was needed to solve the riddle of what that bloke was doing.

Re-locating places in the scrub could be confusing. Out of necessity, Phil had devised a simple way of secretly identifying certain sites. Those that would be worth another look or indicating a track that led to a place of special interest, he cleverly marked. Along fence-lines was easy. A dry stick discretely threaded into the wire mesh would be the marker. However, in open scrub, other secretive measures were needed. Three rocks placed inconspicuously in a group were then used as the indicator. Out on the track Phil collected some rocks and placed them where any unsuspecting traveller would be unable to realise their meaning. Now that the location had been 'sign-posted' Phil wandered back to where he was previously searching for bottles.

On the long drive back home, an inspiration dawned on Phil. 'Instead of putting stones or sticks to mark a spot I should get up-to-date electronically and get myself a GPS,' he noted to himself. Then another thought crossed his mind. 'That bloke probably had a GPS or a smartphone that had one in it and probably marked his location.'

Inclement late-Autumn weather put a halt to any scrub orientated activity for Phil. 'No point in getting soaked or the car bogged, anything made of glass will still be there,' was his dictum. How true was that? One ornately embossed beer bottle that he found lying in the dirt was over 100 years old and still in good condition. To Phil's delight it was now valued at a tidy seventy dollars.

With a bit of help from Barbara, and using the rain as his excuse, he decided it was a good time to clean some of his finds. Together they washed out the sand and other crud from the many collectable bottles and jars that he had bought home. Barbara showed a positive interest in the multitude of different shapes and sizes of those that may have held medicines, lotions, cordials, sauces, potions and poisons of all kinds.

'This one is for my collection, Phil,' Barbara informed him when one of a curious shape or size was spotted. 'And look at this one, it's covered in what looks like Mother of Pearl.'

Phil then imparted some of his recently acquired knowledge. 'Some glassware that has sat in the sun for many years becomes coated in what looks like multi-coloured opal – known as 'opalescence'.'

'Oh Phil, you are so clever,' she said in a pretend little girl voice.

Even though the episode involving the green Hilux continued to puzzle him, other areas were still worthy of a search. One area he wanted to look at was coincidently, about three hundred metres east of where the bloke with the shovel was last seen.

A few days of sunshine reinvigorated his desire to commence searching again.

As he roamed through the scrub, near the same area as before, he found two camp sites. One of recent days and the other would have been active, at least seventy years ago. The humble beer bottle could often be utilised to identify what era a camp was active. 'Pickaxe' brand was the most popular beer bottle in South Australia. Over ninety percent of the bottles Phil discovered were carrying the Pickaxe logo embossed into the glass. On early ones the logo was nearer the base, and later, the circle with the hands holding the 'pickaxe' was higher up, closer to the neck. Some bottles even had the date of manufacture embossed on the base of the bottle. Thus, reasonably accurate confirmation of when the bottle was discarded was possible. At this site a bottle with the embossed date of 1947 was found. Among the finds at the older site he discovered four vintage bottles, still in good condition, that had the baseline date of 1939. To a collector they were worth considerably more than those that had been recently discarded.

It appeared the other more freshly used location, was used for what is commonly termed a 'bushy'. These were camp areas where a group of blokes would gather, to get away from their normal humdrum life. They would enjoy each other's company, often sit around a campfire, drinking, followed by more drinking and a barbecue. Sometimes they would show off their bush-skills, making damper or a meal in a camp oven. Usually, it was just spinning yarns of their past exploits and more drinking. The number of empty beer cans that littered this particular sight bore testimony to just that. Phil crushed the multitude of empty cans and loaded three of his plastic shopping bags with them, then began hiking back to his well-hidden car.

As he walked, he heard the sound of an approaching vehicle above the rustle of leaves as a strong breeze from the northeast began to blow through the trees. 'That's a familiar sound,' he thought and began taking bigger strides, hoping to get closer to the track before the car had passed. By the time he was on the track once more, the vehicle was out of sight. But Phil was not about to give up the chase.

After dumping his backpack containing the more valuable bottles, and the bags of cans into his car, he took a swig of water and started trudging towards the main track. As he did, he heard a different engine sound of another vehicle coming in his direction. Phil instantly hid himself behind some trees, and waited there until the car had passed. It was a late model black BMW sedan. Definitely not the type of car one would go scrub-bashing in. Perhaps they are the same party of beer drinking campers coming out for another 'bushy'.

Phil paused momentarily and wondered if he should go and investigate who was in those vehicles. His curiosity got the better of him. Once again, he followed the tyre tracks. As they did on that earlier occasion, the tyre marks of the BMW had turned off the main track into the same side track as the Green Hilux. It appeared that the driver of the second car was also familiar with the area and knew exactly where to go. However, this time the black car was visibly parked, and no attempt had been made to hide it. Phil could now see the first car was the same green Hilux, just as before, partially hidden in the exact spot it was last time.

Phil was still 50 metres from the vehicles. Loud, irritated, voices came from where the cars were now parked. Both voices had strong accents and often jumped from speaking English to some foreign language. The man he had previously seen was of Middle Eastern appearance and these voices were definitely using language from that part of the world.

Phil crept closer while staying hidden. From his vantage point behind a thicket of trees Phil could now see both men clearly. The new arrival was of similar Middle Eastern type, but was clean shaven and had greased down, combed back, dark hair. They stood about twenty metres apart and their raised voices signified they were not just having a friendly chat. This made Phil nervous and instinct was telling him to 'get the hell out of there.' Once again, his inquisitiveness over rode his sensibility and he began sneaking nearer for a better view.

The soft sandy soil muted any sound of his approach. His heart now pounding, he came to a position where he was able to crouch down and observe the two arguing men. Each standing next to their own car. The BMW was now only thirty-five metres from Phil's position.

'What are you doing here – why you follow me?' shouted the bearded one to his visitor. Then he repeated what seemed to be the same question in the other language, this time with stronger tones.

'Where is it?' The newcomer shouted back.

'You think I have it?' replied the beard. 'I knew you were following me – that's why I tried to hide in here from you!'

Waving his finger at the beard, the BMW driver stated in an angry tone, 'You can't hide from me, I find you easy, I put tracking device on your car.' He then added. 'No more bullshit! You have hidden it here. No more lies, where it is?' he yelled.

The bearded ones face began to turn ruby-red. He extended his arms in the passive 'would I lie to you position' and nervously said, 'I have not got it. It's not here'.

Phil was about to slip away, it was getting too serious for him to stay and watch, then heard 'no beard' say 'I give you one minute, (and something that sounded like 'dakitan wahida'), to say where it is'.

Rather than retreat, Phil foolishly stayed in his position to watch, totally absorbed by what would happen in 'one minute'!

The 'no beard' bloke turned and walked to the left side of his BMW, opened the passenger door, reached in and took something from the glove box.

'Kadhaab, you fucking lie, tell me or I will kill you,' he screamed as he returned to the driver's side of his vehicle once again, now pointing a shiny chrome pistol at the Beard.

Phil dared not move, as his close proximity to the cars was also close to the gun. He was now paralysed with fear, realising the one with the firearm was not in a mood to be stuffed around.

With the gun raised and aimed at the Beard, who was cautiously back stepping closer to his vehicle, he repeated his demand, 'Where is it?' while slowly yet intentionally, moving one step at a time towards the now profusely sweating 'beard', and at the same time waving the gun menacingly back and forth, 'One fucking minute – you just have one minute,' he stated.

The tense scene was suddenly interrupted by a Bronze-Winged pigeon taking flight from a nearby clump of bushes.

Seizing the opportunity of the distraction, the 'beard' lunged towards the driver's door of his ute and flung it open, frantically trying to scramble inside, and grabbing something from the centre console. One leg was still dangling out of the open door.

The gun waving man was now just two metres from the green Hilux. 'I kill you,' he repeated once again. Then without another warning, aimed and fired a shot into the exposed leg that was poking out the ute.

'Aaaarrrgghhh', cried the Beard as he fell from the car, with one hand grasping his profusely bleeding leg. His other hand purposely hiding a handgun he had been able to grab from inside his car. He moaned with pain as his body slid out of the vehicle and dropped onto the ground. Somehow, he managed to keep the firearm hidden under the bloodied and damaged leg.

A stunned Phil heard the shooter say, 'No more chances,' then repeated what possibly was the same demand in that foreign tongue. Then again in English, 'Where is it? Where the fuck is it?'

'If you kill me, you will never find it, so you lose,' moaned the Beard as he attempted to stand up. Once standing with his gun still hidden from sight, with one hand he held onto the open car door, then struggled to turn around to face the other bloke. 'If I die you get nothing,' he painfully repeated.

Without giving any time for the 'no-beard' bloke to reply, the 'beard' thrust his gun forward and immediately began firing shots. Before the other man could react, he had managed to fire several bullets in quick succession, one hitting his greasy haired aggressor in the throat and one finding its target in his head. As 'no beard' fell to the ground his instinctive muscle reflexes, caused his finger to tighten on the trigger and a shot was discharged from his gun. That un-aimed shot, miraculously hit the bearded one directly into his chest and he instantly collapsed forward.

Both men now lay in the dirt and went into writhing, and groaning, blood spewing, spasms. Then almost on cue, simultaneously both ceased movements. Mortally maimed – the pair now lay motionless in pools of their own blood that seeped from their lead-shredded flesh.

An eerie silence cloaked the scene.

Phil's feet were frozen to the ground, his heart rate sky-high as the adrenalin powered through his body. For several minutes he remained motionless, with his mouth agape and eyes wide open in shock. All he could do was stand and listen to himself inhale and exhale heavily, until he could finally begin to move once again.

'Faarking Hell! What do I do? What do I do? Ring the cops? Ring the cops,' he said frantically.

His anxiety level had him almost in tears. He tried to dial 000 on his mobile but failed on the first attempt by accidently hitting 080, then dialled again, this time triple zero, and waited for what seemed an eternity until, 'Police, Fire or Ambulance', came from a faint female voice on the other end.

'Police, police', he stammered.

'Sorry can you repeat that. I can barely hear you,' responded the operator.

'Police' screamed Phil into his phone.

'Is that the Police?' she asked for confirmation.

'Yes, the Police,' the already highly agitated Phil yelled.

'What is your location?' was the next question asked.

'I am out in the bloody scrub east of Tooligie,' Phil replied angrily. 'Just get me the Police,' he demanded.

He became even more frustrated when her next question was, 'Can you repeat your location, and was that Booborowie?'

Unlike the normally calm and usually patient person he was, he blasted the operator with 'just get me the frigging police, will ya?'

After a brief pause, 'One moment sir, connecting you now,' came weakly through his phone.

Rather than stay at the scene Phil fast-jogged back to where his car was hidden, all the time listening for the call to connect with the police. Evidently his phone was drifting in and out of signal range. On arrival at his car, he could see that the phone signal was weak, rising and falling from one signal power-bar to having no bar.

'Got to get the cops,' said the frantic voice in his head. His car wheels spun in the red sand as he reversed out onto the track, then slammed his transmission into Drive. More wheel spin, and dirt flew from the tyres, in the panic of the moment he rammed the accelerator down to the floor.

'Calm down, calm down, before you kill yourself,' he nervously uttered as he gulped a lung full of air and took his foot off the accelerator, slowing down to a safe driving speed. He reminded himself, 'Nothing more can happen, they are both dead, they are both bloody dead.'

As soon as his car cleared the scrub and was on open ground, he checked his phone. It had disconnected. He was about to redial zero, zero, zero when it rang.

'Hello, Constable Williams, Police incident reporting here, are you the person calling about a situation?'

'Yes, that's me,' Phil replied.

'What is your name and what is your location? Can you explain more about the incident?' the officer asked calmly.

His voice had also a soothing effect on Phil. Still with an elevated pulse rate he replied, 'I'm Phil Jackson and I'm just outside of the Hinks Conservation Park on Eyre Peninsula. Just a short distance east from Tooligie. I have just seen two blokes kill each other.'

Officer Williams then began a line of questions, 'Are you in any danger?'

Instantly Phil replied, 'No! I'm safe, they are both dead.'

'Is it possible for you to stay where you are until an officer can meet you there?'

'Where is the copper coming from?'

'The closest unit available will have to come from Cummins.'

'Cummins? That's half an hour away,' Phil advised him.

'Regrettably that is our closest one, he will be joined later by officers from Port Lincoln. In the meantime, an Ambulance will be dispatched from Lock.'

Then the officer asked what vehicle he was driving and if his car could be seen from the highway?

Phil answered, 'Don't worry about the Ambo's. They're both well and truly dead, no one could survive being shot like that!'

Then he described his vehicle. It was recommended that he drive the three kilometres to the Tod Highway and wait there for the patrol car.

'Unfortunately, protocol demands we must have medical persons attend the incident,' Williams advised him, then concluded with. 'The paramedic's will more than likely be the first on scene. They will do an onsite check to verify the deaths or render medical assistance if required and follow procedure at a crime scene. This also applies to you – It is a crime scene and you are not to enter past the point where you observed the incident – do you understand?'

'Yes,' Phil replied, now realising the gravity of the situation.

Phil parked his car at the Tooligie Road and Tod Highway intersection just south of the grain silos and waited. His mind was buzzing with replays of the event and at the same time thinking of what to tell the cops.

'I bet they are going to ask a heap of questions, like, what was I doing there? What time did it happen? Did you know the men?'

Phil rummaged through his glove box and found a pen and some paper. He scribbled a few notes on what had occurred. The time of the incident was easy – that was on his phone when he dialled the emergency number. The rest of the saga he jotted down in reverse order of it happening. From their deaths back to the cars arriving.

Almost twenty-five minutes had passed, then as he reviewed his notes, he sighted the red and blue flashing lights of a speeding police car a kilometre down the highway. By the time it neared, Phil had calmed down considerably and stood patiently outside his car. A rather hyped-up officer jumped from his car.

'Are you Jackson, has the medic arrived yet?' he hastily asked.

'Yes, I'm Phil Jackson. Haven't seen the ambulance,' he replied.

The officer climbed back into his vehicle and began talking on his radio as he took a notebook from the centre console.

'Port Lincoln, Port Lincoln, I am at Tooligie and have made contact with Jackson, no medics in attendance yet, do I wait here on the highway or attend the scene?' he said into his microphone then paused awaiting their reply before he began to repeat his message, 'Port Lincoln, Port Lincoln.' The rest was interrupted by their reply. 'Receiving you Cummins, wait at roadside, our ETA is forty minutes, have just passed through Edillilie. Ambulance has been ordered from Lock, will meet you at your location.'

'Roger Lincoln, Ambulance confirmed, will wait.'

'I reckon it's a bit late for an Ambo,' Phil said nervously as the officer replaced the microphone into its holding clip.

The Cummins-based cop identified himself as Senior Constable Ralph Kusak, then took notes as he questioned Phil while they awaited the arrival of the paramedics. Standard stuff at first, Name, Address, Occupation, car registration and driver's license details.

Then the awkward questions, what was he doing in the area? Did he know the men in question? Did he know why they were in the scrub? Do you have any identification on you?

Luckily Phil had his rego papers in the glove box and driver's license in his wallet to prove his identity.

As his details were being noted, the ambulance arrived. The woman driver and a chap that was seated on the passenger side, both dressed in standard ambo green attire with high-vis reflective stripes encircling their shirts, hopped out. After a brief chat with the officer, they asked Phil for directions to where the patients would be found. With a couple of hand gestures by Phil, to point them in the right direction, and a few hurried scribbled notes they headed off.

Before they left, the officer stated, 'Please remember it is a crime scene. Do not disturb or touch anything but the victims. Your job is to render assistance to them, if they are still alive. From what he has said I doubt if they are.'

As they left, he turned to Phil.

'You might as well get in my car. You can show me the way when the other unit arrives,' he said. In the vehicle, more questions ensued, and Phil was slowly becoming agitated by the repeated questions, 'How do you know the persons, and what is your connection with them?'

'Don't you listen?' Phil shouted angrily, 'I do not know either of them – they just happened to be in the same area as me.'

'All right, all right, calm down. I have to ask these questions. Then he became all officious and began to justify himself by stating, 'The detective will probably ask them all again so I require you to remain calm and give me straight answers. Shouting at me will get you nowhere.'

Phil turned his head, looked the officer directly into his eyes and asked, 'Have you ever seen anyone kill another person? Have you ever seen their blood gushing out of a bullet hole and the look of terror on their face? I have and I am still trying to sort out my brain, so go easy on the lecture.'

'My apologies, Sir,' replied the cop in a much less invasive tone.

'I'm just trying to gather as much info as possible for my report. A major incident such as this, requires a ton of paperwork and the more I get now, means the less time it will take back at the station.' Just as he finished saying that, the officers arrived from Port Lincoln. Both wore ill-fitting suits that had seen too many days of wear. They identified themselves to Phil.

'I'm detective, Smyth.'

'And I'm detective Roberts,' stated the other one as he held out his hand for a shake.

Phil realised he had on occasions seen the shorter one, Smyth, whilst shopping back in Lincoln. Firstly, they spoke to the Cummins based officer, then began querying Phil and taking notes.

'We can't do much here, so we'd better go and see where it all took place. You can guide us to the location,' stated Roberts, the taller of the two detectives.

Arriving at the scene the police could see both bodies still lying in the dirt. The attending Ambo's were sitting in their vehicle looking rather pale. The woman climbed out and joined the detective's as they walked towards the dead men's cars. The female paramedic presented her electronic notepad to Roberts in order for him to view the screen. Her finger pointed at her notes. As she did, she stated in a very 'matter-of-fact' tone.

'Both middle aged males. No sign of life in either. Massive blood loss by both victims – from what appears to be gunshot wounds. From the way the blood had clotted, probably been deceased one to two hours.' The she added, 'Do you want us to transport them or are you going to have a hearse dispatched to collect the corpses?'

'Good question!' replied detective Smyth. 'Rather than have you and your vehicle tied up for hours it possibly would be better if we call up other transport. You can go, but I must remind you, this is a serious police incident, and you must not divulge anything to anyone about it. Thank you for attending.' Then he attempted to use his phone to organise the body retrieval transport.

'No bloody reception here!' he moaned. He then tried calling on the vehicle's radio. 'Lincoln, Lincoln, mobile 4 at Tooligie scene, two victims deceased, please arrange retrieval of two, repeat two, please confirm.'

There was no response. He repeated his message. Once again, no reply. 'Bloody dead spots,' he cursed.

He ordered the uniformed police officer to go back to the road and organise the transport.

'Before you go, put up crime-scene tape here, and across the entry track.'

Phil was ordered to stand back and not come within close proximity of the vehicles. Obediently he stood and watched as Roberts began photographing the bodies from different angles, footprints, number plates and other possible clues as to the events that occurred.

Smyth kept glancing over at Phil as he collected and bagged the guns as evidence, whilst making notations on the bag labels and in his notebook. Then he undertook a search of the victim's pockets, trying to find anything that would confirm their identity and bagging those items as well. He then walked back to the vehicle and placing the evidence items in the boot. For the next two minutes he stood next to the car, looking down and reading his notebook, then strode in a very deliberate manner towards Phil.

Stopping directly in front of Phil he demanded, 'What were you doing here and what is your connection with the deceased?' His dominating voice unnerved Phil. By his tone it was obvious that his thoughts were tending toward Phil being involved in the episode.

All Phil could do was to repeat the events over again, hoping that he would be believed and not suspected of being involved.

After many questions, his version was finally accepted but with a hook attached. 'You will have to give a formal statement at the Port Lincoln Police Station tomorrow and you may also be called upon to give evidence in a court hearing, so make sure you have not left anything out. In the meantime, you are not to discuss this incident with anybody. Are you clear on that? But before you can leave we will have to do a thorough search of your vehicle. Constable Kusak can do that. After that is done we will do a search of the area to ascertain what they, or you, were doing here. Are you sure there is nothing more you can tell us? Now would be a good time to speak up.'

The gruesome episode had turned Phil into a nervous wreck. His vehicle was searched. Apart from his haul of bottles and cans that confirmed his story, nothing of suspicion was found.

Back on the highway, he drove towards home, but it was difficult for him to maintain his concentration on driving. The old railway siding township of Karkoo with an 80kmph speed limit slipped by without him noticing. His mind kept replaying the drama over and over again. As he neared Yeelanna his phone began ringing. Quickly he stopped his car on the roadside.

Thinking it was the police he curtly answered, 'What now?'

'Honey it's me, Barbara, who were you expecting?'

'Sorry, Love,' he almost sobbed into the phone – 'I've had a really bad day. Will tell you all about it when I get home.'

'Why, what's wrong?' she asked.

'Too much to tell you over the phone, I will be home in about an hour. I love you.'

When Phil drove into his driveway, Barbara rushed out to meet him.

'What is it you couldn't tell me over the phone?'

'Let's get inside first and I'll tell you all about what happened,' came his forlorn reply. Now that he was safe once again in his own surroundings, Phil was more composed and was able to relate to her, the harrowing experiences of that day.

Then Barbara raised the big questions, 'What were they arguing about? What did he mean by 'where is it', and why would they shoot each other?'

He pondered her words, and replied, 'Wish I knew!'

Over the next few days, Phil had to attend the police station on several occasions to answer further questions and sign statements. There was no time for anything else in his life.

However, in the back of his mind his thoughts often drifted to the unanswered puzzle of 'what was that man doing there in the first instance, and why was he followed to that same place by the other chap?'

From what he had gathered from the police, they had no explanation as to why. Their reasoning was it may have been a family vendetta, or an item of valuable property may have been involved. They also confirmed their search of the area had been concluded without a result. The mystery remained and irritated him, yet Phil was reluctant to go anywhere near that place. The fear of reliving that horrible drama was too great for him. 'Perhaps one day,' he told himself.

Looking for the elusive historic treasure or finding those antique bottles was now off Phil's agenda.

Barbara realised that Phil, more than ever, needed a distraction. Something that would give him purpose. When she heard that her farmer friends' Red Kelpie bitch had recently had given birth to a litter of puppies, she jumped at the opportunity to purchase one of the male pups. However, her friend advised her, that because the parents were both working dogs, the pup would need plenty of daily exercise.

'For Phil this would be perfect,' Barb said to herself the day she collected the gorgeous red puppy.

'What's in the box?' Phil queried as Barbara struggled to carry her package through the front door.

'Just hold the door, please love, I'll show you when I get inside,' she said.

Obediently, Phil held the door and Barb carried her parcel into the lounge room, where she placed it on the coffee table.

'Whatever you've got in there – it's bloody alive. Hope you have realised – Christmas was last month,' he joked.

With a quick pull of the adhesive tape by Phil, the top of the carton was open. Before Phil could pull back the cardboard flaps, a cheeky red puppy's head pushed its way through.

'It's so cute – boy or girl?' he questioned as he lifted the little dog out of the box. As he did, he copped a shower of puppy wee-wee from what was now obviously a very excited boy.

'Oh honey 'he' is so beautiful,' Phil spluttered as the new arrival eagerly licked his face. 'Does he have a name?' came Phil's next question as he leaned over and kissed Barbara on the cheek.

'That privilege is all yours and that also goes with the obedience lessons you will have to give him,' she giggled.

From then on, most of Phil's days were spent training and exercising his new companion whom he had named 'Tully'.

Barbara had sensitively managed to keep her man from having nightmares or suffer the symptoms of the dreaded PTSD syndrome that could have easily been brought about by the witnessing of the murders.

The daily walks along the Parnkalla Trail became the panacea for Phil to allay the bad memories but also filled the lost passion of his pastime of bushwalking. On these walks Phil could not help picking up the occasional discarded deposit can. Jokingly, he would say to Tully, 'Seems habits are hard to kick' as he stuffed another can into the bag he always carried when out walking.

It was now winter. Plenty of wet days that limited the amount of time for taking Tully for his walks. These days were given to obedience lessons to a very quick canine learner.

As the damp days began to pass, and the sun started to shine a little longer the ever-growing Tully had absorbed everything taught to him over the past months. Then as the days became warmer, the thought of going 'bush' once again stirred in Phil's mind.

'What say we take a drive and I'll show you where it all happened?' he announced to a bemused Barbara.

'Will you be able to handle the memories?' she sensitively

queried.

'Won't know until I get there – I'm going to have to meet those demons one day,' he said in a tone that reflected his hesitation to revisit that place.

'When you are ready, but don't do it if you think it will upset you,' Barbara replied.

'Can't hide from it forever, so let's do it next weekend,' he responded.

On the drive north along the Tod Highway, Phil re-explained what happened the day of the drama. Barbara raised some pertinent questions.

'Why there – why so far from anywhere, and why was the other man using a tracker. Something must be more serious than a family dispute.' Her reservation set Phil thinking. 'Perhaps if we do a grid search we might find the answer. I'll divide the area into six sections. We can do a sector at a time, two pairs of eyes looking and Tully's nose sniffing just may solve the mystery.'

On arrival at the site Phil was hesitant at first and sat in the car slowly moving his head back and forth, trying to overcome his fears. His reluctance to alight from the vehicle was interrupted by Tully's excited barking. The dog wanted out and he was letting his master know. 'OK, I get the message,' he said as he unclipped Tully's harness, then pulled the handle to open the door. 'Come on then Tul, out you get.' Phil lifted his impatient mate from the rear seat of the car while Barb unpacked the metal detector and the map Phil had drawn.

'Righto boss – where do we start?' she laughed to lighten Phil's mood.

'Let's take a look at the closest section first, but I doubt if anything will be found there,' he replied as he pointed to the marked area on his map.

After tracking back and forth through the scrub in the sector, they had found nothing. The only one enjoying the experience was Tully, who was sniffing and cocking his leg on almost every tree. As Phil was about to push aside some branches for both he and Barb to access the adjacent section he asked, 'Will we do the next area now or stop for lunch?'

Tully had no such access problem. He simply pushed his nose through a small gap and squeezed his body through.

'Let's keep going, I'm not hungry yet,' Barbara urged Phil.

Then just as he had finished asking, 'Do we search up and down this way or will we go at right angles to where we are standing?' Tully began barking excitedly. Phil spotted him between the trees, digging excitedly at the soil.

'What ya found mate?' he quizzed the dog as he went to investigate the find.

'What's there, Phil?' Barb asked as she too came to have a look.

'It's only a bloody rabbit hole,' he lamented, then gave the puppy an encouraging pat. 'Good boy, Good boy. Let's go find what those blokes were really doing here.'

They had only walked another fifty metres through the mallee's when Tully began another series of excited barking from the edge of a clearing just a few metres further ahead.

'Where there is one rabbit there's bound to be more,' Phil said with all the confidence of an experienced bushwalker.

But this time, Tully was not after a bunny. He had found something a little more interesting. As Phil approached, he could see the object of his dogs' attention and what was making him so excited. Tully's new find happened to be a rather annoyed Sleepy Lizard that resented being stood over and barked at. With each thrust of the dog's nose towards the grumpy lizard, its mouth would gape wide open, exposing his blue tongue and make a hissing sound.

Phil intervened and growled at his dog in a loud authoritative tone, 'Tully! If it gets a hold on you, it won't let go, so leave it alone. Leave it, leave it!' he commanded his dog.

'Reckon it is now time for lunch,' Barbara suggested.

'Nah, lets finish this bit first!' came Phil's reply.

The excited dog had already raced ahead, sniffing the ground like a bloodhound in search of his next find. Phil scanned the ground for any clue that would solve the mystery.

'Not much here to show us what that bloke was doing. Nothing but sticks, stones, leaves and sand,' Barb moaned as she trudged dutifully behind her man, then added 'Why would a man come out here with a shovel?'

Just as she had finished saying that, Tully once again began yapping at something.

'What has he found this time, a rabbit hole or another lizard?' Phil groaned. But this time the dog was digging frantically at the soil. The toe-nails on his paws were creating a scratching sound.

'He's got something this time!' said Phil, then congratulated the dog with 'Good boy, Good boy, let me see what you have here.'

Phil eagerly scraped at the dirt away with his bare hands. 'There is something here. Honey – looks like a plastic lid!' he exclaimed, then after few more scrapes at the soil, 'Hey, it's the top of a small Esky and there is the rest of it underneath!'

Thankfully the earth surrounding the plastic container was easy digging and Phil soon had the blue, six can sized Esky with a white lid, lifted out of the ground.

'What's in it?' Barb asked excitedly.

'It's got a bit of weight to it – but the lid has been siliconed on. Will need a knife or something that I can use to cut through the seal,' puffed Phil, as he struggled using his fingers to separate the lid from the container. When that did not work, he said, 'I have a screwdriver back in the car, so let's get back there to see what's inside!'

Sitting the Esky on the opened tailgate of his car, Phil attempted to prize the sealant away from the lid. The silicone proved to be tougher than expected, but once the screwdriver had penetrated and split the rubbery compound, Phil was able to pull it from the container in one piece, like a piece of elastic cord. He paused for a few seconds before slipping the locking handle away from the lid.

'Come on – let's see,' Barbara demanded impatiently.

'Just hope it is not a bomb or is booby-trapped,' replied Phil.

'Oh my god – what if it is a bomb?' she suddenly screamed, then added, 'No leave it, let's take it to the police.'

'Bit odd for someone to bury a bomb, but it also seems heavy enough to have one in it – ya never know,' Phil said, while pondering whether to open it or not.

Before Barbara could reply to that, Phil wrenched open the lid and shoved the plastic container to the other side of their vehicle, at the same time grabbing her and the dog and throwing them together to the dirt with his arms around them. For about two minutes they lay still and waited for an explosion. Tully took advantage of the situation of being in a close huddle and gave their faces a sloppy licking with his very wet tongue.

When nothing happened, Barb berated her man as they regained the standing position. 'You stupid idiot!'

'The cops would have to call in the bomb squad if there was the slightest doubt of what is inside. And – what if it the bloody thing exploded on our way home?' Phil said as he held her hand and cautiously walked around to where the Esky had landed.

'Just as I thought,' Phil said as peered at the now open container. 'So, that's what they were arguing over. Figgin' bags of drugs.'

The Esky was tightly packed with 5 plastic bags of a white powdery substance. 'These are definitely going to the cops – we don't what to get caught with this amount, it will be prison for us both if they don't believe we found them. As soon as I get phone reception, I'll call them.'

Phil was instructed to stay at the scene and wait for the Cummins Police officer to come and document the find. Nearly an hour passed before the police car arrived. Time enough for a sandwich and a cup of coffee, and a cooked lamb shank for Tully, that Barb had packed in their own Esky.

Phil recognised the cop as the one that was the first to attend the murder scene.

'Ralph, isn't it?' Phil said as held out his hand as a welcoming gesture.

For a brief moment the officer appeared friendlier this time. However, his demeanour soon changed with questions that placed Phil in a difficult position. He began asking almost the same questions as he had done on his last visit.

Phil made a mental note that possibly it was standard police procedure – be nice at first then get heavy with the questioning.

In an unsympathetic tone Kusak started grilling Phil. 'What were you doing here and how did you find the container?'.

Quick as a flash Phil gave credit to his dog for the find, saying how he found Tully digging excitedly at the dirt.

'We came here so that I could get some closure that might help me stop having the nightmares. Thought a walk in the area might do me some good. Then as we were walking, the dog started barking and scratching at the ground. That's when we found the Esky.'

'So, you were just out for a walk in the scrub and your dog found the container. You know that our police did a search of this same area and found nothing,' the policeman stated in a smug tone.

'Yep, if it wasn't for the dog, we would have not found it either,' replied Phil.

'Righto, you really think I should believe you,' snarled Kusak.

'That is exactly what happened, do you have a problem with that?' Phil replied echoing the officer's indignant manner.

'OK, if that is the way it was, I have no one that can prove otherwise. You will need to make an official statement – for the files, stating just that,' as he hurriedly clicked his camera taking pictures of the site.

'I have enough photos of where you dug it out and all the evidence, so meet me at the station when you get to Cummins, it's getting late, I'm out of here,' the copper said haughtily, as he closed the door of the patrol car, started the motor and shuffled the gear lever into Drive.

As the police car drove away, Barb said, as she looked directly into his eyes 'You fibbed – why?'

'Had to love. He was getting to be a bit obnoxious and if I said we came here to look for what was hidden, I would then be suspected of being part of the murders. And that would have opened a can of worms with me having to prove my innocence,' he offered her as his valid excuse, then gave her a reassuring hug.

'Yes, I could see he was starting to play the big-cop, probably looking for a promotion,' Barb said as she kissed Phil's cheek.

At Cummins the officer's attitude had somewhat calmed. No longer was he the big-deal copper with the attitude that he displayed back at the Conservation Park. He even offered the couple a cup of tea or coffee.

Phil made his statement and duly signed the original and the copies. On instructions from the copper, Barbara had also done the same with her version of events.

'I'll be sending the bags of powder to Port Lincoln for further testing, so you might get a visit from the detectives,' Ralph said, just as they were about to leave.

'No probs – got nothing to hide,' Phil said as they exited the police station.

Early next morning the phone rang. As expected, it was the local detective wanting to interview both Phil and Barbara.

'I'm getting a bit sick of all the hoo-ha that goes with dealing with the police. Seems everyone has to do a report. No wonder they have no time to solve crimes. Their arses are always stuck at their desk filling out forms,' moaned Phil as he placed his phone on the kitchen table.

Once again, the couple repeated their story to the police.

'I suppose Constable Kusak told you that we had several officers at that crime scene doing a grid search – and found nothing. Yet your dog found the drugs. Smart dog, eh!' Detective Roberts said as he looked over Kusak's notes.

After an hour and a half of questioning they were allowed to return home.

'Won't be involving the coppers if I ever find anything else – too much hassle,' Phil stated when they were outside the station doors.

Three days passed and the Phil's phone rang again.

'Detective Roberts here. We've got the results of the tests on those bags of powder you found. Five kilos of high-grade cocaine. Unfortunately, it is unlike any other type of find – you cannot claim it, like you would if you had found a wallet or a watch. Good result and it solves the riddle of what those two were doing in the scrub. Thanks to you, the case can now be closed. We are filing it as a drug related incident.'

'Is that the end of it for us?' Phil responded then added. 'Wasn't me – it was Tully my dog that sniffed it out.'

'Give Tully a big pat from us here at the station – another case solved, thanks.'

For the next three months Tully enjoyed his walks with Phil who was now refreshed from the murder/drugs episode. His mind was settled and he was sleeping much better. Unfortunately. the call of the scrub was gnawing at Phil. His desire to start bottle hunting was once again his focus.

'You won't be going back to that area – will you?' Barbara challenged him.

To which he replied, 'I would love to check out some places that were nearby. Found some really good spots that I think either the railway builders or maybe the water pipeline workers camped. Needs another search, didn't spend enough time looking before. Probably because the scrub was getting too thick to penetrate.' He paused then said, 'Barb, my sweet and lovely partner...'

She interjected. 'I bet you are going to ask me to give my permission to buy that drone you've been looking at on the computer.'

'Can I? Can I?' he laughingly replied.

After a few days of more gentle persuasion, Barb finally relented and gave Phil the answer he wanted – 'you can buy a drone'.

'It is going to cost us heaps? You had better find something of value to warrant buying such an expensive toy,' she cheekily griped and then gave her man hug. 'After what you have been through – you deserve it,' she whispered in his ear.

A local camera store was known for their knowledge about drones.

'From what you've told me, you want a very clear picture of the terrain. I suggest a drone with an onboard high resolution camera would be the way to go,' said the sales-lady.

'If I buy one, can I get some flying lessons with it?' Phil daringly asked.

'Yes, that would be part of the deal,' she said with a smile. The purchase was made, and after several of her lessons he was flying his drone along a nearby beach without an accompanying instructor.

Over the next few days, Phil made some training runs over some similar scrub located nearby at Billy Lights Point.

Here the scrub was much the same density that would be found at Tooligie.

Proudly he boasted to Barbara, 'I've done enough practice and I now feel confident flying the drone. I have also mastered the hang of watching the video screen and operating the flight controls at the same time.'

'I suppose you reckon you're experienced enough to head off to do another collecting expedition. Now with the advantage of your new technology!' she replied.

In a very serious tone Phil said, 'Not sure yet – still a tad concerned going by myself. Do you want to come with me – you know – just in case?'

To which she replied, 'I'm not that keen running around in the scrub anymore.'

Phil then tried to sweeten his plan. 'But babe, it will be different this time. The drone will do the walking for us. All we have to do is watch the screen and if we see anything we just go to that spot. Sounds a lot easier, doesn't it?'

Barb pondered his proposal for a second or two, 'Yes, honey, I'll go – but on one condition. If the drone falls out of the sky – you will go and retrieve it!'

Jokingly Phil suggested, 'Perhaps I should train Tully to do the fetching.'

'And to climb trees,' wise-cracked Barbara.

Rather than go along the same track, to the same location, Phil steered his car through a rarely used, slightly overgrown track that surprisingly veered towards the opposite side of where the drugs were found.

'I thought we were going to a new spot – this track has taken us almost back to the murder scene. That's spooky,' he said while stopped and looking around for an alternate place to go.

'No good sitting here and moaning, Honey – you now have a drone, use it,' Barb needled him as she opened the car door.

Before her feet touched the dirt, Tully pushed his wet nose past her and sprang out of the vehicle, ran to the nearest tree and cocked his leg to have an urgent pee.

Phil prepared the drone for flying, then found an open area to launch his new toy into the sky. With a whirring of the blades the drone shot skywards with ease. Using the aid of the controls and the video screen, Phil flew his drone in a methodical grid search pattern of the surrounding scrub.

After twenty minutes of flights back and forth over the area, 'Stuff all here,' he announced to Barb. 'Might fly it a bit closer to the–' He stopped. 'Where's Tully?'

Back into the sky went the drone, this time to look for the dog. After several minutes Phil declared, 'Found him, found him, the little bugger is having another dig session near where the drugs were found. Bloody hell, hope it is not more drugs. How would the cops react if we found another stash? Reckon I would be shoved in a cell this time. It would take a lot of convincing to prove we had stuff all to do with it. Twice finding drugs, two blokes murdered – tell that to a judge. Bit too much to believe it was a coincidence would be his theory.'

After scrambling through the scrub Phil and Barb found Tully still digging frantically at the soil.

'Good boy – Tull, good boy, what have you found?' Phil said as he patted and rubbed his dog on the head, then began scooping handfuls of dirt away from the buried object. 'Babe – check out this – another white Esky lid.'

'Shit!' Barbara exclaimed. 'If it is more drugs – bury it again. Just don't leave any fingerprints.'

'It's been sealed with silicone, the same as last time. How are we to know what's in it, unless we open it?' Phil replied.

'You're crazy mate, if it is drugs I don't want to know, just get rid of it.'

'But we will never know, if we don't open it,' Phil pleaded.

'Yeh, but look at the shit you would be in, if they suspected you are in any way of being connected to the drugs and the murders. You would be seeing me, looking through bars on weekend visits.'

'What am I supposed to do – just cover it up again, or open it to see what's inside?' Phil retaliated.

Eventually they both realised, the only way to know for sure, was to rip away the silicone sealant and open it up. After several minutes gouging at the rubbery seal, Phil managed to part the lid from the base. Barbara stood as close to Phil as she could, as he prised the lid open.

'What the?' he exclaimed.

The container held dozens of zip-tie bags tightly packed in two rows. Phil tugged a bag from the Esky. Opened the bag and unwrapped the contents. He shook his head in disbelief.

'Not friggin' drugs,' he said as he turned around and showed her what he had. 'Look at this – it's all fifty-dollar notes. There must be at least five hundred bucks, just in this bag.'

Phil started counting the contents of the bag he had. 'Twenty fifty-buck notes, which makes it a thousand.' Then he counted as he flicked his finger over the other bags still held in the container.

'Forty seven, forty eight, forty nine, plus the one I have taken out. That's fifty bags per row. Times that by two.'

Quick as a flash Barb interjected, 'That makes it one hundred bags just in this layer. If they all have the same amount of fifties in them, times that by a thousand. Honey that's a hundred thousand.'

'Struth!' exclaimed Phil. 'Probably at least three layers in the Esky, and if it is all fifties, what does that make it?'

'Three hundred thousand dollars,' she said slowly.

'Faark'n hell,' he blurted as he slumped into the sitting position on the dirt and contemplated the magnitude of their find. Several minutes of silence passed. Each one staring at the Esky packed with bags of money.

'Well – What now? What do we do with it?' she said seriously.

'If we bury it again – someone else might find it. If we take it with us and get caught with it – we will be in deep shit.' Phil responded.

'What if we bury it in another place?' Barb suggested.

'Might as well put it back here – same thing – it may be found by someone, Tully found it with his nose so the odds of another dog sniffing it out would be high, let's take it home. At least we will know where it is,' he responded.

'Clean the dirt off and wrap it with that canvas and stick it on the back seat. Put the drone on top of it,' Phil ordered.

Dutifully Barb obeyed her man. Then he turned his head towards his dog that was already sitting on the back seat. 'Tully, my mate – don't let anyone touch it. Got that, and if someone does, I'll blame you. You were the one that found it. If your nose was less sensitive, it would still be buried! So, guard it, or you will end up doing time in the dog slammer,' he nervously joked.

TURN RIGHT AT TOOLIGIE

Their mood was subdued while driving south down the Tod Highway. Both in quiet contemplation of what to do with the cash. As they neared Cummins their nerves were set on edge.

'Shite,' exclaimed Phil, as his heart started thumping, 'Bloody cops ahead and he has already seen me. Too late to turn around and there is no side road we can go down.'

The local police paddy wagon was parked diagonally across the road in front of the Lutheran Church and the officer was holding up his hand to signal the car to stop.

Then Phil whispered. 'It's bloody Ralph Kusak with a road block. What in the hell does he want? There is no way he would know about the cash. Don't say anything just leave the talking to me,' as he came to a stop in front of the copper.

'Phil, isn't it?' the Constable said as he poked his head through the driver's window then looked at the back seat. 'Been flying a drone?' he said.

'Yep,' Phil replied. 'Barb bought it for my birthday. Just went out to give it a run,' countered Phil.

'No drugs this time?' the officer joked. Before Phil could reply, Ralph made a quick change of subject and advised them that a road-train loaded with grain, had tipped over at the other end of town just past the caravan park and was blocking that exit from the town. 'If you want to get to Lincoln tonight you will have to go via Tumby. The cleanup will take hours,' the officer said, then threw an unexpected curve ball. 'Find anything?' and looked at what Phil guiltily thought as suspicion.

'Nah,' said Phil – 'still learning to fly it.'

Their conversation was conveniently interrupted by the loud hiss of air brakes as a truck pulled up behind Phil's vehicle. The

Constable then walked towards the truck to advise the driver of the road closure.

'Get the hell out of here,' Barb insisted. 'We have an Esky loaded with cash sitting on the back seat. If he asks us to show what is under the canvas we are screwed.'

After clicking his turn signal for a left turn, Phil drove over the railway crossing and headed towards Tumby Bay, keen to distance themselves as far as possible from the law.

Back at home in Lincoln, Phil parked his car as close to the house as possible, hoping this would conceal the removal of the 'Esky' from the back seat without being sighted by his nosey neighbours.

'Where are going to put it? We can't leave it out in the open,' Barbara said as Phil carried the Esky through the back door.

'I was thinking about that all the way home. Best place is somewhere we rarely go. I reckon I'll stash it in the back of the spare room wardrobe for now – need a bit more time to make a plan for somewhere long-term,' he replied.

'What plan?' she said looking directly into his face.

Next day Phil went out to the shed to retrieve the tape measure he was using last week. As he came back into the house Barb re-asked her question.

'What plan – that needs a tape measure?'

'Got to see if it will fit – so need to measure before I cut,' he replied as he began pulling back the spare room carpet.

Phil measured between the rows of nails that held down the floorboards. 'Four fifty – take off the width of the bearer that makes it about four ten he stated as he opened the robe and placed

44

his tape across the Esky lid. 'Fantastic – Three eighty. That leaves enough for the plywood box. Reckon we can hide it here it here under the robe. Even I wouldn't think to pull back a cupboard to look for something. Especially a robe full of junk.'

In the following days, Phil busied himself in the shed making the plywood box to hold the Esky. His inquisitive, retired, neighbour Ernie, watched him for a while – over the fence, until his curiosity got the better of him.

'Watcha makin' mate?' the old bloke asked.

'Just a junk box – got a heap of stuff that we don't use but is too good to throw away,' instantly replied Phil.

'Yeh! Me too. Perhaps we should hold a garage sale one day.'

'Great idea – make it a combined one?' Phil suggested in return.

'Leave ya to it,' the neighbour said, then walked away.

'Nosey old bastard,' was Phil's immediate thought.

To hide the noise of the jigsaw that he was going to use to attack the floorboards, Phil asked Barb to take the old Ghetto-blaster outside and do some of her aerobic exercises, like she used to do a couple of years before.

'That will give the old bugger plenty to perve on. Barbie dancing around the lawn, in her Lycra. The loud music will cover any noise I make,' he chuckled to himself, then had another worrisome thought. 'Let's hope he doesn't whine about the music.'

Just as Phil predicted, old Ernie positioned himself in his garden where he could sneakily watch the scantily clad Barb do her workout, bending, stretching and dancing to the music. His concentration on her body made him totally unaware of Phil's electric jigsaw munching into the floorboards.

Phil's measurements were spot on. His plywood box fitted snugly between the floor bearers. The Esky also slipped easily inside the underfloor container. With the aid of some Tek screws the cut-out floorboards were joined together and hinged on the underside and made into a lid that that worked like a trap door.

Phil gave the thumbs up sign to Barbara when she came into the room to inspect his handy work.

She hugged him and said, 'Your plan for me to distract the old codger from next door worked. I could see him hiding behind a tree watching everything I did. Just to keep him interested I did some sexy stretches, and he fell for it.'

The carpet was repositioned and the robe slid back into place.

'No one would think of looking there,' Phil said, then paused. 'We don't know exactly how much is there,' he said to her.

'Who cares, it's ours now,' she quickly replied in a serious tone. 'Let's just forget it for a few weeks and go about with our normal lives. Spending a large amount of cash will raise plenty of suspicion. We don't want a visit from the cops – do we honey?'

'Great idea love – it will give us time to think about how to make it part of our normal income. A few wins here and there on the pokies, lottery or horses would cover any extra cash-flow.'

Barb immediately retorted angrily, 'You not going to gamble with it – that will be the quickest way to lose the lot.'

Phil retaliated, 'It was just a thought. A mate of mine explained how heaps of 'dirty' money gets 'washed' through the casinos by some Asians and drug dealers that needed to 'launder' illicit cash.'

'No way – we are not like those criminals,' she growled.

One evening, almost three weeks later, Barbara asked the question. 'How much money did you think is in the Esky?'

Phil shrugged his shoulders and scratched the back of his head before answering, 'At least three hundred Gee, that's if they're all fifties and not smaller notes.'

'Are we ever going to count it?' she asked.

'No hurry, we don't urgently need it. You have your job at the supermarket and I am still selling car parts, so why start spending just for the sake of it? If it was a million bucks or more we might think of moving away and living somewhere it's always warm and sunny.'

Another month slipped by.

The chill of late autumn was beginning to make itself known.

'Time we went and cut another load of firewood. Better do it this weekend before the rain starts,' Phil announced, then added, 'I'll ask Bob at my work, if we can get a trailer load from his brother's farm at Wanilla. I could see from the highway, they have a pile of old sugar gums they cleared from a fence-line two years ago. It should be dry enough to burn now.'

The roar of Phil's chainsaw covered the sound of a police paddy wagon coming to a stop on the outer side of the fence. Constable Kusak got out the wagon and walked up to the barbed wire and tried to attract Phil's attention. Barbie saw him first and over the noise, pointed so that Phil could see they had a visitor. Phil shut down the chainsaw and took off his earmuffs.

'G'day Phil,' said the copper and then stated what was blatantly obvious, 'Getting yourself some firewood?'

Phil's quick response was, 'Too bloody expensive to have it delivered ready cut.'

Then Ralph continued, 'Recognised that it was your ute, so I pulled up to let you know the latest about those two dealers you witnessed being killed. Seems there was also a heap of cash that went missing around the same those blokes turned up over here.'

For a moment Phil felt sick. He began having thoughts that he was now going to be arrested and taken in again for questioning. Barbara was thinking much the same and reached out and took hold of Phil's arm and stood close by his side.

Thankfully, the copper went on to say, 'So a team from the Major Crime Squad did a search of the area. Pity your dog, what's-his-name, could not smell money or he would have found the container of cash, buried just a few metres away from the where you found the drugs. Nearly one hundred and eighty grand packed in an old suitcase wrapped in plastic,' then added cheekily, 'Looks like you dipped out. That amount of moolah would have bought you a lifetime's supply of wood. Just for your information – the money has been impounded as being part of the illegal drug trade, so it goes back to the government.'

Trying to hide their spontaneous sighs of relief, Phil joked with the officer, 'If you lend me a couple of fifties I'll start teaching Tully how to find hidden money.'

Life for the couple went on as usual. The cash still untouched and well hidden under the floor, the lure of wanting more bush adventures began entering their conversations.

'Honey, how about taking next weekend off and we will go have a look at the Gawler Ranges. Might find some old stuff up there,' he asked her with a hug.

'Nah, can't! Silvia is going on holidays for a week, so I have to work the weekend. Perhaps the weekend after we can go,' she replied.

'If that's the case love, I will go and do a bit of fossicking in Lincoln National Park. There was an old stone building that was once home to a shepherd and what's left of some sheep yards nearby. Might find a few coins.'

Barbara giggled at his suggestion. 'You're going to look for coins?'

'What is wrong with that?' he retorted.

'There are thousands of dollars in the box and you want to find a few more pennies. You could buy an entire coin dealers shop with that sort of money.' She laughed then gave him a big hug in return. 'I love you so much, babe.' She kissed him.

The question of how much money was in the Esky niggled at Phil. It often kept him awake, his mind wandering through options of what to do with their find. His curiosity was also shared by Barbara.

'Perhaps we should count the cash to know exactly what is there,' she suggested to him as they lay in bed, unable to sleep, while listening to the late night ABC Radio quiz.

'If we count it – what next? Do we then start having the urge to spend some and risk getting caught? Perhaps we should have handed it in, then we would not live in fear of losing it,' Phil said as he propped himself on one arm to look directly at his bedmate.

Barbara rolled towards him and touched his forehead with one finger. 'I know there is a lot going on in your head. It's been ages since you had a good sleep. Maybe we should hand it in now and get the demon off our back.'

'Shit no!' Phil retaliated. 'That would be admitting we withheld evidence and I could possibly go to prison for that. Looks like we are stuck with the loot. All we have to do is find a way to use it without getting busted.'

Over the next two weeks ideas were swapped on ways the money could be spent without raising suspicion. Neither Barb nor Phil could come up with a foolproof solution. It was suggested by Phil that they pretend the money did not exist, and life would be emotionally easier. Then they could get some much-needed sleep.

The money remained in its cubby hole under the wardrobe.

No matter how hard they tried, it was the subconscious torment each had to contend with. It took all their willpower to resist the urge to take it out and start counting.

Selling auto parts over a counter became a drag. When business was quiet, Phil's mind would wander, thinking about being involved in something more exciting than car parts.

Perhaps if they moved house to live elsewhere, some of the cash could be used to make life more pleasant. That way Barbie could do her study to get a degree in Art, which she always spoke of doing. Maybe buy a big four-wheel-drive rig and go bush to metal detect for gold.

Then reality would smash that idea, 'What if we got caught?' The money would be confiscated, and we would we have to go to prison.

Then another voice in his head would counter that line of thought and reply, 'It was only drug dealer's money, nobody lost, and the cops have found some, so in their mind it was the only cash there. The druggies have gotten their fix and it is only the two dead dealers that have missed out, but they are now dead so what is the problem?'

Phil dwelt on that reasoning for a few moments then the ghastly probability crept into his thinking.

'What if those two owed the cash to another dealer higher up in the drug trade? Would they come looking for it?'

That thought sent a shudder down his spine.

'We can't afford the risk so the cash stays hidden,' he immediately concluded.

The mere thought of a third party coming to look for the cash was making Phil paranoid. As he went about his daily business, subconsciously he was now on constant alert watching out for anyone that may possible be a 'dealer' that was looking for the money.

The old adage of 'think it and it will happen' became a reality for Phil. While shopping at a nearby supermarket he had an eerie feeling he was being watched. At the end of the biscuit aisle, Phil spotted a person looking his way.

Unfortunately for his nerves, the man that he saw, looked similar to one of the murderers. Stocky with a beard and having a Middle Eastern appearance. In panic, Phil dropped the basket of food items that he had collected and headed for the exit.

Not waiting see if he was being followed, with his heart thumping loudly under his shirt, climbed into his ute and hastily drove out of the carpark. As he drove, much of his focus was on his rear-view mirror, constantly checking to see if he was being followed. As an added precaution he decided to park his vehicle at the rear of the house, where it could not be seen from the roadway.

'Why are you parked on the lawn?' Barbara quizzed. 'Gonna give the ute a wash,' came his immediate response, hoping not to raise any suspicion from her.

'Aren't you going to shift the car off the lawn?' Barb asked as it neared the time to begin making the evening meal, and added 'Where is the stuff I asked you pick up from the shop?'

'Whoops – sorry love, I forgot to get it. We'll have to have something different for our meal tonight. Something healthy for a change. My fitness level needs a boost. Healthier food and some exercise won't hurt either of us, for a while. I reckon I'll ride my bike to work for this week,' he declared to Barb.

'Why the sudden change?' she laughingly responded.

'Just doing what I should be doing, looking after myself. It was you that said I'm getting a bit of a beer-gut. I am going to get fit to please you, my dear.'

'Are you really doing it for me? – how do I know it is not for another woman?' she retorted.

'Barbie Babe, everything I do is for you,' he replied as he gave her posterior a quick pat.

True to his word Phil rode his bicycle to work for the next few days. On his bike he continued looking over his shoulder to see if he was being followed.

One night he dreamed of riding his bike and being chased by someone in a car. It was a crazy dream. No matter how fast he pedalled, the car was staying close behind. Just as a gun was being brandished at him through the vehicle window, Phil woke suddenly gasping for breath.

'What's the matter honey?' Barbie sleepily asked.

'Just a bad dream love, go back to sleep,' he reassured her, trying to keep his fears from upsetting her as well.

Three cold months slipped by without a mention or thought about using the stashed booty. The couple went to their respective jobs and life seemed almost normal again.

Phil busied himself with remaking the vegetable growing area. He assembled three raised garden bed frames and set them in place, and over the next few days filled each one with fresh soil.

In the meantime, he continued to remain on alert, vigilantly watching to see if his dream of being followed had any substance to it. Anyone remotely resembling the drug dealers he would eye with cautious suspicion.

After a while his fears subsided and he regained a semblance of being relaxed, but still maintained his keep fit routine of riding the bike to work. That was until a cold snap and rain dominated the local weather and the ute once again became his preferred mode of transport.

The chilly night air required the remaining amount of the wood they had collected to be burned in their slow-combustion heater.

The fire would usually keep burning well into the late morning and the house would be kept warm throughout the day with the air control vent shut down. Hot ashes would often linger in the fireplace. The fire could be easily relit by whoever came home first in the evening.

Barbara had decided to go home to have lunch instead of eating in the supermarket staff room.

'I'll just pop another piece of wood in the heater, before going back to work,' she thought.

Unfortunately, there was only a few hot ashes remaining in the firebox. To ensure the log would burn Barbie slipped a firelighter cube under the material she had placed on the coals. For a few minutes she waited, watching through the glass door of the heater, until a flame appeared. Satisfied with her task, she then went back to the supermarket to continue her afternoon shift.

That afternoon the supermarket was unusually busy.

'Barbie, there's a bloke named Ernie wanting to urgently speak to you,' Kathy, the front of shop supervisor called out to her. 'What in the hell does that old pervert want – tell him we are too busy and I'll talk to him when I get home this evening.'

'He says it cannot wait until then, it's urgent.'

Barbie asked herself 'what in the hell could be that urgent?' as she picked up the store's phone. 'Hello Barbara here, can I help–' and before she could finish her sentence an agitated voice hollered through the phone.

'Ernie, your neighbour here, you had better get home. Your house is on fire! I've called the brigade and they are on their way. I have your dog – he's safe with me.'

'Shit! Our house is on fire!' Barbie screamed as she slammed down the phone and rushed up to the supervisor. 'Got to go – find someone else to take over my position will ya,' Barb said in panic as she rushed towards the staffroom to get her car keys without waiting for the supervisor to reply.

By the time Barbie had arrived back at home, part of the back section of the house was well ablaze. Fire brigade officers were spraying water from two hoses to try and save what little was left of that area of their home.

Phil came screeching around the corner in his ute but was

forced to stop four houses away, the road blocked by one of the two MFS firetrucks that were attending the scene. The rear bedroom of the house was engulfed in flame. He joined Barbie on the roadside.

'Stand back,' ordered one of the firefighters.

'It's our house,' Barbie pleaded with him.

'You have to keep out of our way – stand back, stand back,' he ordered them.

Reluctantly they both retreated several metres away and watched as the flames were being extinguished.

Eventually the fire was put under total control but unfortunately the damage had already been done. That section was now just a mess of charred timber. The fire had totally destroyed the rear bedroom and the spare room.

Barbara was clinging to Phil, sobbing her heart out.

'Our house, it's burnt – we have lost the back rooms. What are we going to do?' She buried her wet face into Phil's shirtfront.

'Thank heavens we have insurance. I wonder what caused it,' Phil responded in a matter of fact tone.

A sudden emotional fear swept over her. 'I put some wood on the fire before going back to work at lunchtime,' her voice quivered.

'Did you shut the heater door?' he quizzed her.

'Yes, I'm sure I did. I waited until the wood started to burn again. Yes! I did shut the door,' she said in a positive tone.

Phil answered, 'Might have been an electrical fault. Was anything being recharged.'

'Yes,' said Barbara in a sheepish mode. 'I,' she paused and looked him directly in the eyes, 'I put your drone batteries on charge so we could use it this weekend. They were on the table in the back bedroom. I was hoping you would show me how to fly it.'

Phil put his arm around her. 'Perhaps that wasn't the cause. We'll have to wait until the Fries do their investigation. But for now it is important that we get in touch with the insurance mob as soon as possible. Find out what we have to do.'

Barbie pushed Phil's arm away, grabbed his hand and forcefully dragged him away from the proximity of the others that were gawking at what was happening to the house.

'What are you doing?' he asked with a puzzled expression.

'The money, the money. After all the stress we have gone through, what if it is burned and what if they find any trace of it?' she whispered to him, so no one else could hear.

'Bugger the money – where is Tully?'

'Don't worry, honey – Ernie has him, he's safe.'

Relieved, Phil then replied, 'The money – it's not there. I shifted it.'

Barbara stared directly at him, then asked angrily, 'What have you done with it?'

'It's safe. Don't get your tits in a tangled,' he replied.

'Where is it?' she demanded.

'Let's talk about that later,' he said, then put his arm around her again and stared at the fire.

Temporary accommodation was arranged by the insurance company in a local cabin park. Next day, the fire investigators did their search.

A few days later a letter of explanation arrived.

'Our investigators attended your property after the fire. As a result of their findings,' it read, 'A battery charger unit was confirmed as the source of the fire'. The note went on – 'Due to a fault in the charger, the batteries more than likely overheated and burst into flame. This was not the first one of its make to do it. A recall of the chargers was ordered but not yet made public. Hence no fault was due to neglect by the homeowner.'

Thankfully, it was Phil's drone recharger to blame and not due to Barbara relighting the fire. However, the house needed fixing. Luckily for the couple, the local insurance agent had, after the report came through, organised for a builder to start immediately on the repairs.

With her hands on her hips Barbara confronted Phil and demanded, 'When are you going to tell me what you did with the money?'

Phil sat her down at the small table in the cabin kitchen, held her hand and began to explain.

'I had a dream that I was being chased by some drug dealer's thugs, and they followed me home. Then they broke into our house and started beating me. They tried to force me to tell them where the money was hidden. In the dream, they kept punching me until you shouted 'Stop! Stop! I will tell you'. I know it was only a dream. Rather than say anything that would scare the hell out of you, I thought it better to secretly shift the stuff to someplace you did not know.'

'Will you tell me where it is – or is it better I do not know?' she asked.

'Honey, it is up to you if you want to know. But if something ever happens to me, and you don't know the location – what then? Your choice.'

'On that basis you had better tell me,' came her rapid reply as she stood up next to him.

'Let's put it this way – if you ever need to dig the rhubarb out of the raised garden, don't dig too deeply,' Phil told her with a smirk on his face.

Barbie broke into laughter, 'You are such a wonderful and clever man, no wonder I love you so much.'

'Love you too honey,' he said, then responded with a lingering cuddle and a kiss to her neck.

While repairs were being carried out by the builders, Phil went daily to feed the dog and tend to his plants in the raised garden bed.

One of builder team made a joke of his attention to the garden. 'Do you really love gardening or are just keeping an eye on us?' Little did he know the real reason for Phil coming each day or his extra attention to the Rhubarb. A month later the house had been passed as being liveable, much to the couple, and Tully's, relief.

The Jackson's life once again returned to what could only be described as almost normal. 'Almost' – because of the stash that was hidden in the garden. Although Phil's fear of being hunted by a drug dealer looking for the money, had lessened, he continued to be cautious and on the lookout for any stranger that was acting suspiciously.

After many discussions, and each one putting forward a multitude of options of how they might use the money, it was decided that contrary to spending, it would be wise to bank as much of their wages as possible in order to create an illusion of them having money. This would provide an alibi so that any extra cash spent would not give reason for someone to question their wealth. Having money would then appear to be the result of hard work and saving.

However, both Phil and Barbie had no illusions as how long it would take to create such a wealth base. With that in mind, watching the account balances grow became a fun game for them.

When everything seemed to be going well, Phil was suddenly bought back to reality when he was at the newsagent shopping for a birthday card for his beloved Barbara.

A man corresponding with Phil's now paranoid and dreaded Middle Eastern appearance stood at the magazine stand and occasionally glanced towards the greeting card section instead of looking at the publications in front of him. His appearance and his actions un-nerved Phil.

Rather than selecting a card Phil quickly grabbed the closest one and headed towards the check-out counter. Unfortunately for Phil, the man had chosen a magazine and was also headed in the same direction. This needed evasive action.

With a quick turn away from the counter by Phil, he now positioned himself at the lottery ticket sales section.

'Can I have a quick-pick for the Thursday draw?' he requested while trying not to look in the suspicious man's direction.

At the same time as the sales girl was attending to his request, tapping on the point-of-sale computer screen, the man was then next in line to be served at the adjacent counter.

Holding the lottery ticket in her hand, the sales girl said to Phil, '$22.50, thank you sir.'

As Phil went to hand over the money he asked her, 'Who is that bloke?' While discretely pointing his finger in his direction.

'Oh – that is the new head priest at the Catholic school. He has only been in Lincoln for two weeks, I'm told Father Romero is his name. I can take your money for the birthday card as well,' she answered while extending out her hand.

'Yes, please do,' a much-relieved Phil replied, while adding another ten dollar note to the cash he was holding. Phil walked away from the counter, then placed the newly folded lottery ticket into his wallet. It was at that moment it dawned upon him, that he was still jumping at shadows and very suspicious of any person that looked similar to the dead men.

'Seems I can't even distinguish a priest from a drug dealer,' he chuckled to himself.

Sunday morning, the Jacksons were lying in bed, listening to the radio and taking it easy. Tully had positioned himself on the foot end of the quilt. He was enjoying the game of nipping at any toe movements made by Barbara and making growling noises to add to his delight.

The local news came on. One of the items grabbed Phil's attention.

'The Lotteries Commission has not yet been able to locate the winner of last Thursday's Power Ball. The unregistered ticket was sold in a Port Lincoln Newsagency.' Phil made a mental note check his ticket next day.

Luck comes in many ways. For the Jacksons, perhaps it was finding the stash of money. Unfortunately, that was not without a psychological cost. The drama of the actual shooting, the close shaves with the police and the constant fear of being caught, dampened any supposed 'luck'.

Monday came and went.

Phil had been busy and forgotten to check his lotto ticket. On Tuesday morning the chatter at his workplace was all about the mystery local lotto winner. His curiosity was spiked. He deliberately made time to go to the agency and check the ticket he had in his wallet. After digging through a mass of hoarded receipts he eventually found a lotto ticket.

'Must get rid of those bits of paper,' he said to himself as he withdrew the ticket from his wallet and placed it under the scanner. 'Congratulations, your ticket is a winner, you have won $309.50'.

Even though it was a nice amount, Phil's heart sank. Seems it was not him that won the jackpot.

When he passed the ticket to the salesperson behind the counter, she casually remarked 'not a fortune on this one – but not a bad win', as she handed him his winnings.

Little did he realise it was an old ticket that he bought last month and had never checked.

The local news continued to announce, the mystery winner had not come forward to claim their prize.

After a sleep in, Sunday was generally washing day for the Jacksons. Clothes, sheets, towels and whatever else that needed to be put through the washing machine.

Barbara was a stickler for ensuring all pockets were empty. The mess caused by bits of fluffy white paper over everything that was just washed, due to one facial tissue, really peeved her. Thus, as a habit, all pockets were checked for the dreaded forgotten tissues, and the occasional small denomination coin.

'Got any more clothes that need washing?' Barbie called out from the laundry.

'Just my jeans,' he replied.

'Bring them to me, if you want them washed today,' she ordered.

The routine of checking pockets proved once again, that Phil had left something in his pockets, actually, two items. In the left hand pocket, the dreaded tissues and in the back pocket was his wallet.

'Mmmm,' she said to herself, 'what has he left in it for me?' as she opened up the folds. 'Looks like I get the money for my shopping today.'

'Phil,' do you want your wallet washed? I have taken out the money – we don't launder dirty money here, babe,' she jokingly called out, just as Phil entered the laundry room.

'No need to shout,' he said, holding his hand out for his wallet. 'I see you have already taken some of the cash – you could have taken out all those old receipts and sorted them for me.'

Little did he know that Barbie had spotted a lottery ticket among the receipts and had already removed it, so that she could check if it had won a prize.

With the clothes washed and now hanging on the clothesline, she had the time to check that ticket. On her smart phone she had an app for the lottery results. Flicking through the last few games results, she came to Thursday's Power Ball numbers.

With a pen in hand, each number that came up was circled.

'Got that one, and that one, that one too, that one, and that one. That's five,' she said with excitement. 'Need one more, and the Powerball.' Then for a moment she froze, not believing what was in her hand. 'Phil – come here!' she screamed.

Regretfully their ticket did not have the 'Powerball' that was needed to win the jackpot of 40 million dollars. Their share was division two – a very respectable three-hundred-and-ninety-eight thousand dollars.

'Luck' had once again flowed their way in the form of a winning lottery ticket. The same ticket Phil purchased whilst trying to dodge the man of 'Middle Eastern appearance' was a winner.

Now the couple's biggest problem was keeping the win a secret. Under lottery rules the larger prize money could not be collected for two weeks. At Phil's request their names and address were not to be disclosed by the Lotteries. Even though were trying hard not to reveal their luck, it was extremely difficult for them to hide the big smiles that adorned their faces.

Jokingly, Phil would proudly show his $309.50 winning lottery receipt to anyone that suspected them of being the Jackpot winners.

'Now that we have got our own money coming, perhaps we should now hand in the cash to the police?' Barbie suggested.

'Definitely not,' he replied sternly. 'It will still implicate us in a police investigation – they would ask, why had we not declared it at the time it was found. I have a much better idea.'

Over time, it was speculated on the grapevine that the Jacksons had won some money but nobody was sure of just how much. Small town gossip usually exaggerates just how big the prize that was won and by whom.

Just in case any suspicions abounded that linked the Jacksons with the win, Phil kept showing his three-hundred-dollar winner to anyone that asked. This would keep the gossipers guessing. Nobody really knew if they had won or not. It was no longer an issue for them.

The joy of not being found out pleased the couple. Bearing this in mind, under the cover of darkness, Phil dug up the rhubarb plant and exhumed the Esky from its hiding place in the garden. With curtains pulled and all doors locked, he did the count.

Coincidently the contents of the Esky tallied up to just over the $340,000. Close to what Phil had speculated the day they found the buried Esky.

Now that his curiosity was sated, the container and the cash was stashed once again, under the floor in the newly-rebuilt spare room.

Having a win on the lotteries gave them cover to use the drug money. Phil realised the amount of the 'win' money was very close to that of the 'find' cash. That money however, was tainted by the murders and the connection it may have had with drug dealers. Rather than using it for themselves, Phil devised a plan to secretly give donations to charities that dealt with drug rehabilitation, homelessness and other groups that helped to repair broken lives. Drug money going to aid drug users – and this was drug money.

'That's brilliant, honey,' Barbara responded when he told her of his plan.

'We have more than enough for ourselves of our own. So that heap of cash will gradually be donated over time, let's start with a sizable gift to a local cause. But no one is to know it was not from our winnings,' he confided.

In due time a charity was selected. Discreetly $10,000 of the money had found a worthy cause without any fanfare or seeking publicity.

To celebrate the start of their now being an altruistic couple, they dined at a local hotel.

Whilst waiting for the main course to be served, they (and everyone else in the hotel) watched in amusement as a police car pull up outside the hotel's front window.

'Wonder who they are after, they look serious?' a bloke from an adjacent table jokingly said.

His question was answered when two policemen walked up to the Jacksons table. One, in uniform and the other in plain clothes Phil recognised as detective Roberts, who had contacted him some time ago and told how the police discovered what Tully had found, had now been identified by the laboratory as being a stash of illicit drugs.

Phil went pale, Barbie reached out and clasped his hand. Both dreading to hear what the cops may have to say.

'Can you both please come with us,' the policeman stated in a tone that made Phil even more nervous. His mind concluded that the cash he had just given to the charity must have somehow been traceable. Flanked by both officers, Phil and Barb walked, gripping each other's hand, towards the awaiting police car. Once outside, Detective Roberts asked them to take a seat in the back. Leaving the other policeman outside, Roberts climbed into the driver's seat and swivelled himself as to look at his passengers.

He informed them that he knew where the donation had come from.

Phil's heart was almost pounding out of his shirt, his mouth went dry and his breathing rate escalated.

The detective looked at the couple with a deliberate 'got ya' stare then spoke. 'I was at the bank today, when I noticed the administrator from the drug rehab centre was banking a sizable wad of cash. I wondered where such an amount of money might have come from. After questioning her she disclosed that it was you that gave the money.'

Then his mood suddenly changed. He turned his face away and looked out over the bay for a moment and said nothing. Then turning his head back to look directly at the couple, he took a deep breath and began to speak.

'I hate drugs, drug dealers and anyone else connected with the supply of illegal drugs.' His lecture clearly aimed at the Jacksons and unnerving them to the point where Phil was almost about to confess, that the money was part of the cash they found near the drugs.

Then Roberts turned his head further and looked Phil directly in the eye, and stated in a serious tone.

'We have always had our suspicions about you. Firstly, you were there at the double murder scene. Then 'your dog' supposedly found the drugs in the same area. Circumstantial, yes! But we still had our doubts. Now, we want know where the donation cash came from.'

Both Phil and Barbie thought an arrest was imminent. Then the detective started more of his lecture.

'You made the woman from the rehab centre promise not to tell who the donor was. After a 'small' threat of her being arrested, she let out your secret.' He continued, 'It would be better for us to continue our discussion back at the station. I assume you have your car here. Then both of you, get out and come to the station in it.'

Whilst they drove the short distance to the police building

Barbara unintentionally added to Phil's mountain of concerns,

'They have got us this time – haven't they love? What are we going to do?'

Pulling up to give way to an approaching vehicle at the round-about, Phil watched the other car as it passed then quietly said to his wife, 'No – I don't think so. If they were convinced we were involved with those two drug dealers, they would have arrested us on the spot. Not given us a chance to get away in our car. Honey, say as little as possible – let me do the talking.'

'Thanks for coming here,' the detective said as he showed them to a seat in his office then sat himself on the other side of the desk.

Just then the phone began to ring. He answered it and paused. With hand gestures he indicated to the police officer with him, to take the call in the other office. After the officer had left the room, he swivelled back and forth slowly yet deliberately on his chair, while chewing on the end of a biro, saying nothing.

Roberts looked at the pair in a rather puzzled way.

It was a long moment that passed before he spoke.

'You might be thinking, what evidence does he have that links the cash donation with the drug dealers? You are right if you believe there is none – except for a rather large donation to the charity from a couple of low paid workers.' Roberts stood up from his chair and walked deliberately towards to the other side of his desk looking directly at Phil as he did.

'I have always thought it was strange that, you – the murders, the drugs, always seem to be connected. Yet each time there has been a plausible explanation that got you off the hook. However, I had accepted that was the case. But now a wad of cash has suddenly emerged. What am I to think – eh? I would be delighted to know how you had such an amount of money.'

Phil sat thinking for a moment, then turned his head as his eyes followed Roberts as he walked back to his chair and sat himself down.

'Please explain,' the detective said, mimicking the female politician that famously used that phrase in Parliament.

'I suppose you have heard that a winning lottery ticket was purchased in Port Lincoln? We have tried to keep it a secret,' Phil paused for a moment, which gave Roberts enough time to interject.

'What are you trying to tell me – you won the lottery, but up to now have kept it a secret?' The detective threw his head back and laughed, 'You want me to believe it was you that won the Jackpot? First thing tomorrow I will be checking your story. It had better be true. Forty friggin million.' Shaking his head in partial disbelief he rose once again out his seat and went back to Phil.

The detective's moment of disbelief came to a screeching halt when Phil told him, it was only division two and not the jackpot that they won. Phil shuffled through his wallet and showed him the lotteries receipt.

'Three hundred and ninety-eight thou – you had a windfall of nearly four hundred thousand, no wonder you can give away ten thou, you lucky bastard,' he said shaking his head in amazement.

Then without warning, the previously dominant detective, that was implying that the couple were involved with the drugs episode reached out and shook Phil's hand.

Tears filled his eyes before softly saying. 'I'll keep the secret of your big win, if you keep mine. My son is a recovering ice addict. He gets counselling at that place. Your wonderful donation will go a long way to help him and the others there that have been involved in using drugs. Thank you so much – I am sorry I doubted you.'

On the drive home, Barbara, who had kept quiet through almost the entire interview turned her head and looked towards Phil, then quietly spoke, 'Honey, I know you did not lie to that detective, but you never exposed the truth either, did you?'

Phil took his left hand off the steering wheel reached out and gave her right thigh a gentle squeeze.

'Yes love – I deliberately never lied. When we won the lottery money, I made up my mind never to spend any of the cash we found, for ourselves. I also promised myself not to let the police or another illegal dealer, ever get their hands again on what we found. Who knows where it could end up? Back in the drug scene, buying more drugs or possibly ending up with the money going into government general revenue. Only to be wasted on new furniture or new carpet in some overpaid bureaucrat's office. This way it will give us a project that we can do. It will be up to us to figure out which charities need financial help and ensuring they get it. We will be turning drug money into actual assistance money. Money that came from the wrong side of society. Money that now can benefit others.'

Phil stopped the car, then reached out and held Barbara's hands and looked directly into her eyes.

'Today we make a promise... Never to splurge any of that Esky money on ourselves. We are only to use it in ways that will help lessen the insidious pain caused by drugs and has wrecked so many lives. And – we do it in a way that keeps a low profile on our giving.

Cos what we do not want is some pissed off drug dealer to come looking for us. We definitely, are not wanting to make the headlines. I hope you agree!'

'Agreed,' replied a smiling Barbie, sealing her pledge with a spontaneous kiss on Phil's lips. 'You are a wonderful man, Phillip Jackson. That's why I love you so much.'

They carried on homeward, but, just as the two were beginning to relax, their comfort zone was given an unexpected shake by the flashing of red and blue lights reflected in the car's rear-view mirror.

'What the heck, what do they want now?' Phil cursed out aloud as he watched a police car approaching at speed.

'Perhaps the cops have other evidence or realise there is more that happened and not what you have told them,' Barb said nervously as she turned her head towards the on-coming patrol car.

Phil anxiously monitored the patrol car as the two cars were now traveling side by side.

His heartrate had already skyrocketed. He could see that there was only one officer in the overtaking vehicle.

Looking directly at Phil, the policeman took one hand from the steering wheel, then made several repeated motions with his fingers pointing towards the roadside to indicate for Phil to pull over.

'Bloody Roberts, he's sent the copper to do his dirty work and arrest us. He's always believed the drugs were ours and we were dealers. Looks like the mongrel has got us now.'

'Better pull over Hun, or we will get done for failing to stop,' Barbara nervously suggested as she watched the police car pull over and come to a halt, thirty metres ahead of them.

With an air of panic, Phil complied, 'Like I said, don't say anything, tell him bugger all. If someone has to confess, I'll do the talking, and I will take the blame for everything, that way we can keep you out of prison.'

When Phil's car had also come to a stop, the policeman stood for a moment outside the patrol vehicle, deliberately adjusted his hat, and then strode with authority towards the now very nervous couple.

'Remember, let me do the talking!' Phil hissed through his teeth so the copper could not see that he was giving instructions to Barb, as he pushed the button to wind down the driver's side window.

Even though he was trembling internally, Phil pretended to be calmly innocent as he addressed the policeman that was now standing alongside his door. 'Good evening officer, was I speeding?'

'No mate, I am just returning your reading glasses. You left them behind at the station.'

He handed them to a very relieved Phil through the open window.

'Thanks.'

Phil and Barby clutched hands and sighed in unison as they watched the policeman walk away.

www.ingramcontent.com/pod-product-compliance
Lightning Source LLC
Chambersburg PA
CBHW070647120726
47909CB00004B/1615